"Who are you?" A small voice seemed to whisper through the darkness.

Heart still racing, she reached out and pulled the cord. With a click, the lamp on the nightstand beside her bed snapped on, illuminating the room, the almost barren, square coffin-like room, that in that moment felt like a familiar friend. The room was sparsely furnished, just like the other rooms in the colony.

"More of these weird dreams. At least they are consistent with their strangeness." Tera said to herself, slowly calming her breathing.

Continuing to take steady, deep breaths, she ran her still-shaky hands through her long, dark hair, still matted from sleep. Sitting up on her tiny cot, she stared at the wall for a moment, longing for just a simple night of good sleep; one with no dreams. She only knew one way to get that, and it wasn't time yet. He would meet her soon. As her body began to relax, her pulse slowed, and she felt sleep whispering its sweet song to her, like a lullaby, and she began to drift again.

Tera stood in a place that looked like it was made entirely of marble, except for a door. The door looked as it was carved from pure gold. It was radiant and almost glowed in stark contrast to the rest of the room. The door boasted the most splendid and intricate designs, unlike anything Tera had ever seen in her life. A thick, frothy mist churned near the floor, rolling over her ankles, and across the floor of the room.

The room was empty, except for the mist, herself, and the one big, golden door. The walls of sleek marble protected the nearly windowless circular room. Above, a skylight let in gentle shimmers, and a soft glow of indigo and amethyst that illuminated the room. Tera found it a magnificent sight. The ceiling looked as if it were meticulously carved out of the marble, the skylight spanning the entirety of the room. Through the skylight shone the galaxy in all its glory.

Once again, Tera felt that yearning deep in her core to be among those stars. With that yearning, she also felt a rising sense of frustration. These dreams, and stupid space, had been plaguing her for over a year, and every time, it was always something different but still similar.

Two things now struck her: this was the first time she had heard any voice or voices when these questions were asked of her, and secondly, why start asking her questions in the dreams now, after a year of showing her nothing but the stars and galaxy? So many questions, but all she really wanted was sleep and an end to these silent but beautiful nightmares.

"If you are going to question who I am, then I will question why I keep having these weird dreams." Tera said out loud, hoping the voice would speak to her again. Maybe if she could talk to it, she could see what the host of these dreams wanted.

A loud clunk followed by a pop and swoosh of air shook Tera out of her angry state. The seal on the golden door popped and slowly began to open. Mustering all of the determination she could to find answers, she strode towards the door, imitating a confidence she did not feel. As she neared the enormous door, she could hear soft crying from the room within. Her pulse began to speed up.

All at once, Tera jolted awake. Her eyes shot open as her heart raced in her chest in the lit room. Its warm glow comforted her and made her feel less alone. Frustrated and exhausted, she kicked her legs as she rolled out of bed and onto the hard concrete floor.

Shortly after getting out of bed, she stepped out of her dorm room. Tera was fairly tall for her 15 years of age, her shoulder-length dark hair had been roughly brushed. The dark green button up jumpsuit complimented her dark eyes and olive skin. She scratched at her arm and pulled at the rough fabric of the jumpsuit. The suits were not the most comfortable, and they seemed to be made of some sort of itchy fabric that, without undergarments, would make the suits unbearable. The lace-up boots made it easy to navigate the debris from the recent expansion of the colony. Her shoes were well worn, and the leather was cracking in places.

She stretched as she walked through the long dormitory hall of doors leading to multiple rooms, her boots making a soft thumping noise with the occasional crunch of rocks or debris under her boots. Dorms just like hers. Each room held a Colonist. There were about 100 Colonists in total. Their ages ranged from 12-18, and of all different walks of life. The only connection they had to each other was that they were orphans that the colony had taken in, except for Tera. Walking quietly down the darkened halls while they slept at this early hour, Tera felt bad for the other kids growing up without any adult influence, other than the lessons given by the colony classes.

As far as Tera could tell, the main purpose of the Colonists was to learn to read and write sufficiently to be able to file away the growing stacks of files and papers. No one explained to them why exactly they were doing it, but just that it had to be done. When questioned, the colony staff would look at them coldly and say something like "*it's an honorable task to keep humanity going.*" What a bunch of dead, printed trees meant to the survival of humanity didn't make sense to many of her fellow Colonists, but they did as they were told. As for Tera, she enjoyed the research and, looking back into a world they never knew.

"You finally made it. I was about, to give up on you." Said a voice in the darkness as she approached the spot.

"Well, there's a first time for everything." Tera said smugly, sitting on the floor of the alcove in the tunnel. Her irritation seemed to melt away when he was around, helping her to let go of the dreams and the frustration at their current situation. The sound of water dripping off of a distant pipe echoed from the darkness of the hallway.

"You weren't spotted by anyone, right?" The voice asked softly in her ear.

"Nope, not a one." She smiled.

"Did she show up again?" She asked, looking the boy next to her full in the face. Kaiden Lewis was a few years older than Tera, with dirty blonde hair, green eyes and fair skin. He was taller than she was by a lot. Their friendship had started because they shared something; something that no one else had experienced.

"Yeah, she did. It was just more of the same." Kaiden said with a sigh, as Tera leaned her head on his shoulder.

"Did you have another dream?" Kaiden asked after a moment of silence.

"Yeah, two actually. And someone spoke to me." Tera said.

"What? Really? What did it say?" Kaiden asked in a excited whisper, turning to face Tera in the darkness.

"It said 'Who are you?'" Tera said, in a mock ghost voice. A shiver ran down her spine, despite her joke.

"That's kinda creepy for a mysterious dream voice," Kaiden said with a glimmer of hope in his eyes.

"I'm hoping to find out what it wants and why we keep having these experiences." Tera responded.

"Oh, man! I wish the crying girl would talk. She never says a damn thing. I've asked her many questions, and it's always the same. She just stands there in the corner of my room and sobs. A little sobbing girl made up of stars." Kaiden said, running hand through his hair.

"You know, when you put it that way, it sounds so silly," Tera said, poking him in the ribs with her elbow.

"Down right annoying, if you ask me." Kaiden said, a smirk crossing is face.

As their conversation died down, the exhaustion of the night's events began to wear on them both. Slowly, they began to drift off into a dreamless sleep to the sound of the slow rhythmic drip of the pipe.

The steady rhythm of the heart monitor began to beat slower. The ticks on the screen became more and more shallow, and the beeping slowed until finally it blared a loud noise as the line was perfectly flat. The patient was dead.

"This one has failed," James Ward thought to himself, his hands still in his blood-covered surgical gloves. A burning anger began to fill him. His body began to shake with a ferocity, like a raging fire boiling over. Time was running out for him. For all of them. James removed his gloves as he watched the blood fade to a light pink circle, down the drain.

"We will get it right next time, Sir." Said a voice from behind him. He turned to see his assistant wearing surgical scrubs and goggles. He was covered in blood just like James. Except there was a coldness to the man's tone, and he didn't like that.

"Next time, huh." James said, then in one quick turn he grabbed the younger man by the throat.

"Next time?" James hissed "Soon it will be too late. We need it now. " He glared with an unearthly stare into the mans eyes. James held the man by the throat, and could feel his tendons tensing as the man tried to gasp for air and pulled frantically on James' arm. The younger man's eyes began to bulge, and his face turned a faint blue.

James released his grip, and the other man collapsed to the floor, heaving and gasping, for air. Other members of James' personnel began to rush into the room and take the assistant away. James stood still. He had to control himself better. But even now, he could feel his mask slipping, a mask which he barely held on to even now.

Taking in a deep breath to compose himself, he turned to the body in the middle of the room. It was that of a boy, about the age of 10 years old. His hair was dark and skin was pale.

He would never see another moment on this Earth.

The operating room always had a green cast to James' eyes. It was good sized windowless room with an operating bed in the middle of it. The heart monitor and other tools were next to the bed. The drain underneath the bed on the floor was for moments like this: to help with the clean up, though James never did that. He had heard it was helpful. With one more look at the body on the table, he strode out of the room, shaking his head.

"Running out of time." He muttered under his breath, as the door softly clicked behind him.

Standing in the hallway, almost as if at attention, a small group of people in hazard gear stood off to the side. The clean up crew were thorough and good at their jobs, unlike some other personnel. The cleaners were single-minded in their devotion to the cause: vital research for existence in the colony. James applauded them for that. Nodding a hello, he walked past them, keeping his mind on the one thing that had been driving him for all of these years since the attacks on Earth: the survival of the species.

Tera and Kaiden woke to the sound of buzzing down the hall, their dreamless rest giving them a little rejuvenation for the day's tasks ahead. Tera stretched as Kaiden yawned loudly.

"Ladies first." Kaiden said, letting Tera walk ahead of him by a few paces, just enough to be suspicious. The tunnel-like halls began to fill with their peers coming out of their rooms, dressed in the same jumpsuits as Kaiden and Tera.

The other kids laughed and greeted their friends. Tera smiled to herself listening to them. If having those weird dreams were somehow able to keep the others from harm, then it was worth the cost. Lightly shoving her, Kaiden rejoined her, putting on his best acting face.

"Good morning, Miss Tera-bow-berra spacing out in outer space land," he said with a chuckle, patting her on the shoulder.

"I'm not spacing out, just in deep contemplation about the meaning of life, ya know." Tera replied, with a grin and a light shove.

The two began to walk in step with each other. The hall was getting crowded as they all moved towards the dining hall. For the most part, the hallway was empty of rooms, except for the Lab, which took up most of right part of the hallway. It was one of the bigger rooms, with multiple rooms inside of it. Not many people were called to go into the Lab. The ones that did never came back. The personnel always said that they were runaways.

"How could you run away from a underground place made up with tunnels and no real exits?" Tera thought to herself. Sure, some of the kids in the beginning had tried to rise up against the colony Personnel and attempted an escape. One female worker was killed in the incident but the rebel kids were never heard from again, or so the colony rumors go. For the most part, it had stifled the courage of the Colonists to stage another coup. On occasion, there would be a kid that would try, but they all ended up the same. They would be called into the Lab, with a summons by James Ward. They would never be heard from, again.

"Move it freaks," a voice said loudly, as a body slammed into Tera's shoulder, knocking her into Kaiden. Tripping over her own feet, and partially over Kaiden, Tera fell to the ground. Kaiden managed to catch himself on the curved tunnel wall. The group of people walking by cackled with their leader, a skinny, tall, freckle faced, blonde haired girl who gave Tera an evil glare as she laughed with her friends.

"Nice one, Nora!" one the blonde-haired girl's cronies called as the group made its way into the dining hall.

"What a bunch of jerks." Kaiden said, as he helped her up off the ground. She dusted herself off. Tera nodded in agreement to Kaiden, with a determined annoyance.

Tera looked at the group as they disappeared into the dining hall. Nora Martin was considered popular, not only for her charms, but also her cruelty. It was only natural for someone who appeared to be slightly different to be made the scapegoat, Tera thought to herself. Even with that small bit of wisdom, it still hurt. Scratching unconsciously at her arm, she began to walk towards the dining hall as her stomach growled in a loud protest.

The dining hall was a square room with a surprisingly flat ceiling and floor. The walls were a pale cement grey and the floor matched. Tables and chairs were scattered about in a haphazard sort of way in the larger space, where the Colonists who arrived first began to sit and eat as they chatting with one another. On the right was a long metal bar with trays and different-sized containers for the food. It was always the same: runny cold eggs with limp bacon and a powered type of orange colored juice with which to wash down their morning pills.

Kaiden nudged Tera. "Smile. It'll really set her off. Trust me," he said in a whisper, as he got his tray.

The metal tray clinked on the metal bar as a worker slopped out some runny lumpy eggs on to his plate another placed the limp bacon. He grabbed the orange juice and pills and placed them on his tray, Tera doing likewise.

"How could I possibly smile at a time like this," Tera thought, staring moodily at her reflection in the orange juice. Their usual table was in the farthest corner in the dining hall.

The silence between to two of them could be called reflective but still comfortable. Tera lifted the orange juice to her lips as she noticed something stuck under her pill container.

Curiosity filled her, wiping away her gloom for a moment, and she almost slammed down her glass as she picked up the pill container. Under the container was a note stuck to it. She pulled it off and opened it.

It read "*Don't trust everything they tell you. The pills are killing the powers inside you.*"

CHAPTER
2

Oscar Ward was late. His arthritis-ridden hips ached in protest at his speed. His heavy work boots sloshed in the ankle high waste that filled this part of the tunnel from rain water and garbage that had not been collected yet. Why they wanted to meet here in this vile tunnel was beyond Oscar's understanding, but when you were a simple man like Oscar, you followed orders. The tunnel was dark, with the exception of the small bit of light from the trash shoot that he had crawled through to get here.

Finally reaching the meeting place, he hurried up to the figure standing in darkness, the figure's eyes mere pinpricks of light. The figure had a smell to it, like a musky cat that had rolled around in a garbage heap; a stench that seemingly overpowered the garbage chute.

"You are late, Mister Ward," the being said with a somewhat musical, mocking tone to its voice.

"I know, I know. It's the curse of old age. I apologize, Sir." Oscar said, rubbing his hip out of habit. Truthfully, his arthritis wasn't entirely to be blamed for his tardiness. He was starting to get cold feet about this meeting. Unconsciously, he rubbed his hands on the back of his bald head.

"You have kept us waiting. We don't like to wait. We almost canceled our agreement with you." The being trailed off.

"But no matter, you are here now." It spoke this time in an almost feminine voice as it moved, and seemed to pull something from its abyss-like figure.

It produced what looked like a small feather in its dark smoke-like hand. To anyone else, it would look like an average feather. But Oscar could see it. A glimmer of what looked like galaxies upon galaxies of stars in the threads and strands. Oscar gingerly took the feather in his hands, cradling it like the last child on Earth. He looked up at the being in shock.

Trembling, Oscar said "I… I thought they were all extinct. I thought they all died off in the great war 8 years ago…"

"There are a great many things you know not of, Mister Ward." The being replied, now in an aged man's voice riddled with wisdom, but also, near death. "You must keep a close eye on that son of yours. He is hindering our plans."

"James? He knows nothing of what I do, of what we do, for the benefit of mankind. What's left of it, at least." Oscar said in a near panic. Perhaps James' research could be delayed a bit longer, he thought to himself.

"We will take your word, Mister Ward. Next time, tardiness will not be tolerated." It said, in the soft voice of a child, and vanished like a candle snuffed out.

Kaiden Lewis sat in the worn, white chair. It was cold in the white, sterile room. He was still in shock over the note that had been under Tera's pill container. He of course took the note's strange advice, though now, his hands had begun to shake. The walls had once been white, but the flooding on this floor of the colony had eroded the paint. Its once white walls were now stained with dirt and grime, giving the room an eerie cast. Most of the rooms in the Lab were like this or worse. It was the way the council saw fit to terminate the rebels, and now those stains were a reminder of its history.

"Do you still get the visions, Kaiden?" Asked an older hispanic woman sitting facing him in a small folding chair with a clip board. Rubbing his hands together, he sat forward in the nearly ancient chair, looking away from her.

"No, not really." He lied.

Amy Gomez looked at him with a knowing gaze.

"The dark circles under your eyes have been improving the last few weeks. Have you been able to get better sleep with those meditation techniques we talked about last month?" She asked, clicking her pen twice and scribbling something down. It didn't matter what, she wrote, or even if her pen touched the paper, it still made the client nervous enough to keep talking, Amy mused with a wry grin.

Kaiden flushed slightly and coughed in his hand out of nervousness, remembering his early morning naps with Tera. When they first started, it was out of desperation. Now, he found that most nights, he couldn't wait until the crying girl showed up so he could see Tera again.

"The meditation, oh yeah. That helped a lot." Kaiden said, still avoiding eye contact.

The "crying girl" he called her, because that's what she did. She would stand in his room at night crying. He tried everything to console her, which admittedly was a impossible thing for him to do. She looked as if she was a shapeless form made up of millions of stars, and her eyes shone brightly, one indigo and one amethyst. She never said anything, just stood in his room, crying from about 1 a.m. until 3 a.m. In the beginning, he thought he was going crazy.

That's when he started leaving his room at night. He had found Tera one night, coming back from the bathroom, and they were able to connect about her dreams and his visions. Maybe the girl he saw and Tera's dreams were connected somehow. Kaiden wondered what not taking the pills would do. Would it affect the crying girl and the visions? He was eager to find out.

Amy Gomez smiled weakly at the boy sitting before her in the room. This was their 15th meeting, and he was very coy about letting on about his visions in the last 10 meetings. She had a feeling he was talking to someone else about them, which for herself and the council was a very bad thing. They couldn't have the children talking amongst themselves about these visions and visitations. They just couldn't have that at all. It would ruin everything.

"Well Kaiden, I am pleased to hear that the meditations are helping you sleep better at night." She said, clicking her pen three times and writing a note. Kaiden looked up at her for the first time this meeting. He grunted a response as was normal for most boys his age. "Thank you for this meeting, I look forward to seeing you again next time. Next, time lets talk about your memories." She said with a probing grin.

He looked at the aging woman with a glare that would freeze a hot coffee.

"I told you I didn't want to talk about it."
He said, and stormed out of the room. As the
door slammed, Amy smirked and clicked her pen
three times and wrote another note.

"He's almost ready." It said.

Tera worked in Archives. For most of her
peers, who were about her age it, it was a boring,
menial task. Not for Tera, she greatly enjoyed
learning the history of the colony and fueling her
own theories of what had happened. Which
excited her to no end. Even with her excitement
about research, she couldn't help but wonder how
Kaiden was doing in the Lab and what not taking
her morning pills might lead to.

The archive room was a large room filled
with tall metal shelving. Most of the shelves were
half full of neatly organized papers, binders, and
folders. They held mostly newspaper and
magazine clippings, sometimes the occasional
print-out, on the attacks that happened. There
was a whole other room that was filled with
papers in less neat stacks that needed sorting and

to be put away. The flood really had messed up a lot of their hard work, destroying some files.

Their task was to go through the files and catalog them into chronological order. They would tell them that it was important for the colony to see where they came from and keep good records of where they were going as a community, but there were very few articles older than seven years old, and even those were greatly damaged with wear and water damage from the flood.

Tera made her way to today's stack of papers. The stack in her hands was large and not neatly shuffled together, which, made it more difficult to carry. Sighing, she heaved the large stack up, leaning it against her body for support. She could make two trips, but she was far too stubborn for that.

Turning towards the desk for sorting opposite of her, she felt her foot catch on something. Before she knew it, the papers flew out of her hands, scattering everywhere. She fell to the ground, papers flying around her as she fell.

Groaning, she sat up, rubbing her knee, and looked up to see no one else but Nora Martin. Nora hovered over Tera, hands clasped in fake sympathy.

"Oh! Did that hurt?! I didn't see you there, freak!" Nora said mockingly, as she tittered along with her small group of what Tera deemed Nora's twiddle dee and twiddle dumber. Tera glared at Nora and her crew, the two girls with Nora seemed more parasites of Nora than individuals. They mimicked Nora in her body language and even in her tone of voice. Tera never remembered getting their names. Though Nora towered over the two girls, she seemed to do it as a Queen greeting her peasant, not a gangly awkward sort of way.

Twiddle dee was a blonde girl on Nora's right. She had shoulder length hair, and was petite with bright amber eyes. Twiddle dumber was taller than Twiddle dee but not as tall as Nora. She had raven black wavy hair, with pale skin and ice cold blue eyes.

Nora and her twiddle twins skipped away, skidding up loose paper that Tera had dropped to fly back into her face.

"Why do they always do this kind of stuff?" She muttered to herself.

"Wow, that was rude, are you okay?" Asked a small voice next to her. Tera turned to the source of the voice to see a petite asian girl smile kindly at her as she started gathering papers next to Tera.

"Yeah, I'm okay." Tera said, brushing strands of her hair away from her face, and began to pick up papers.

After a few minutes of silence, and with almost all of the papers neatly stacked on the floor in a nice pile, Tera cleared her throat.

"Um, are you new, I have never seen you here in Archives." Tera said looking, at the slight asian girl with long silky black hair and dark eyes.

The girl gave a big smile and put out her hand. "My name is Yun Chang. I just got transferred to Archives from Childcare."

"Childcare, huh? Thats a pretty tough one. Dealing with all the new kids." Tera said thoughtfully, as she finished gathering her papers, and began to walk with Yun to begin the task of putting them away

"It wasn't as bad as most people think. I really got attached to a lot of the kids. They come in with so many problems, but compassion can go along way to help mend some of them." Yun said, reflecting on her time in child care. "The hardest part for me was when they had to move on from child care to formal lessons. I miss them still." She said solemnly.

"Some of those kids should be entering jobs soon, right? So, you'll get to see them again?" Tera said, trying to sound supportive.

"If they survive the Lab tests. Not many do." Yun said, staring off at nothing, seeming to remember her own testing.

Tera shivered.

The testing for her was one of her first memories, and worst. As if by reflex, Tera's heart began racing and breath quickening, she could feel her chest tightening with anxiety. The straps were just so tight on the operating table, and she wanted to break free. They all wanted to break free.

The millions of voices which screamed in her head and her body began to pull away slightly from the operating table as someone barked out for an injection into the stint in her arm. Hot liquid rushed into her body, and things settled back down. All she was left with was a galaxy of stars and a pair of eyes which contained those stars. Indigo and Amethyst, they shimmered.

"Who are you?" A voice echoed in her mind. This wasn't a flash-back, it was something new. Perhaps a side effect of not taking those forsaken pills?

Gasping and blinking hard, her vision began to clear, and she tried to focus on Yun's confused face.

"Whoa! Hey! You're okay, just breathe." Yun said in a hushed whisper, while rubbing Tera's shoulder softly. Tera was crouched on the ground, almost in a fetal position, her skin damp from sweat. Catching her breath as her vision of the room cleared, she stood up slowly with Yun's help.

"Thanks. It was just a silly flashback. I haven't had one of those in a long time." Tera said, trying to cover her lie.

Steadying herself, Tera looked down at the last piece of paper in her hand. It read *"Project Beyond The Stars."* Her main job was to look at the date stamp only and put it in order according to log number and date.

Ordinarily, she would have put it away by now. Find the date and shelve it. But not this one. One name stood out to her, clear as day: *Oscar Ward.*

CHAPTER
3

O wen Benson stood with his age-weathered hands clasped behind his back. The room was circular with tall windows that let in the morning light. On the walls hung tattered shreds of fabric, torn and scorched almost beyond recognition; the scraps of the once-revered flags of the nations of Earth that remained as a symbol and reminder to the council of all that had been lost.

As the other council members entered the room, wearing mended suits and dresses of days past, Owen wondered to himself how the fools found time to mend their clothing. The council members varied in age and race, though most of them showed the effects of the tremendous stress they had been under since the attacks.

The deal Owen had made, which saved humanity itself, and ended of the attacks, would certainly allow him to live on past his years here on this Earth. Perhaps they would even raise up a statue in his honor, Owen mused to himself as he spotted a familiar face taking their seat across from him. Owen smirked to himself as his eyes lingered on Amy Gomez. She quickly looked up at him having felt his gaze. She shot him a quick glare as she flushed and exited the room.

The council members were all seated. Owen, still standing, cleared his throat and smoothed out his khaki jumpsuit.

"Thank you all for coming today on such short notice. I know it was a long trip for a few of you from the farther colonies, but it will be worth it." He began. "We have an honored guest today." He said, stepping aside as a dark figure made of up what seemed to be a dark murky smoke and a million stars stepped forward from the shadows.

Where its eyes should have been, instead shown six stars, three on each side of its smooth, diamond-shaped head, filled with a shifting mist. It lacked any sort of mouth, and communicated with some kind of telepathy. Its form was long and slender, with two legs and two arms almost of equal length allowing it to shift easily from walking upright to running on all fours.

· The being stood before them on its long legs, and stooped down to avoid hitting the ceiling of the council room. The council members looked at the being with a mix of terror and awe.

Owen cleared his throat nervously. He may have been the one to make to deal with these beasts, but they still made him nervous, especially since they had torn apart the Earth in their frantic search for the ones they hunted.

The being surveyed the room, swishing its large head from side to side, seemingly to take in the room.

"Aelore activity has increased. Why is this?" The being said with a thousand rattling voices speaking at different times, but all sounding at once. The council members covered their ears, though the sounds resounded only in their minds.

One woman looked up at the being as she dabbed a slow trickle of blood that came from her nose and down her top lip. She was a woman of 77 years old. Her soft white hair had been pinned back in bun. Her shining eyes looked up at it.

"We have no reports of new activities." She said as calmly as she could manage. "Sir." She added quickly, staring into its strange eyes.

It seemed to blink, then its head twitched in a snap as it got closer to the woman.

"We are giving the reports, Human," it hissed

with a high pitched squeal that caused the other members to scream and cover their ears. Some of them hid under the large table. "Did we not bless this pitiful planet with a season of peace? Are we not your saviors? Who else would have saved you from killing this planet with your wars? Starvation and poverty are no longer in existence with us in control. All we ask is to turn over all Aelores to us." It bellowed now, in a guttural roar as the members of the council began to scream, blood began to run on the floor as the each member bled from the eyes and nose.

The Silore looked on at the dead council members. Human lives meant nothing to it. All it wanted was the full extinction of its ancient foe, the Aelores. Then, it seemed to vaporize into the darkness, leaving Owen to step back into his secret room. He smiled, pulling something from his pocket: a small feather with a million galaxies of stars in it. He looked into the room, now void of life except for his own.

"Fools. Now our real work can begin. No more hinderances." Owen said, as he looked out the window at the bright stars in the night sky.

Kaiden stretched as he walked towards archives. He hated those therapy sessions. The hallway was silent except for the rhythmic thumps of his footsteps on floor. His thoughts were consumed with the mysterious note. What did the pills really do? As he pondered these questions and more, a new sound accompanied his foot steps, a sound so familiar he almost didn't catch it.

The soft sobbing of a young girl grew louder and louder. His eyes widened as he turned around to see the crying girl. He called her. She stood in front of him with her hands over her eyes, tears like falling stars fell onto the ground in a spark of light. Her form was made up of swirling indigo and amethyst, with a shimmer of twinkling of stars. Her hair was an ever shifting array and twisting, shooting stars.

"What the…" Kaiden whispered, as he knelt down in front of the girl.

The girl sniffed, lowered her hands, and looked up at him with her mismatched eyes filled with galaxies. An ancient wisdom of eons past seemed to pour from her eyes. Her eyes brimmed with twinkling star tears.

"Won't you save us, Kaiden Lewis?" Her voice was sweet and innocent, but there was a haunting quality to it that sent a shiver down his spine.

"*You and I are the same, Kaiden*" The girl said, as her small hand touched his face. His eyes widened as a rush of images flooded into his mind, until it was filled with an image of a planet, like a swirling beautiful marble in a distant galaxy with twin moons. He seemed to sail through the atmosphere of the planet. The sky was a soft lavender, and the twin moons illuminated eerily.

"My species are known as the Aelores in your language." The crying girl seemed to speak, but only in Kaiden's mind with a soft, childlike voice that resounded with a thousand years of wisdom.

"Our true name would liquify your mind if you were to attempt the pronunciation. We Aelores were a peaceful species, focusing on philosophy and the creative arts as our basis, with our leaders, the Eternal Loirial."

Kaiden could see buildings that floated into the sky, made up of soft curves created from a shimmering marble-like material. Beings of all shapes and colors bustled around the buildings. Some looked almost human, while others looked like many different parts of animals but yet walking upright. There were also others that walked on six legs, or slithered like giant slugs towering over the other creatures.

"Many different species from around our own solar system would come to our planet to seek knowledge and culture, to lead the life of a scholar, rather than a farmer or a warrior, as many of the other planets surrounding us had made their professions. This left us nearly defenseless, as we considered war to be a thing of the past. Our small fleets were nothing compared to what they brought upon

us."

Suddenly, a large laser beam broke through the atmosphere in a streak of white light. The explosion was such that he would never forget. As the dust and smoke cleared, he saw that city was gone, and body parts of creatures, scattered everywhere.

A massive, dark fleet filled the broken sky like a gathering storm. "The Silore." Kaiden whispered, recognizing the ships from news clippings.

"When the Silore attacked us and destroyed our beloved planet, it was our duty as the Eternal Loirial to flee and retain what knowledge we had to build again."

Kaiden saw two small children holding hands and running, though their forms were blurry, as though he was looking through a fogged mirror while the rest of the vision was crisp. As the two ran, large beings with six legs chased them. The beings seemed to be part shadow and part thick smoke, while retaining a solid form. Panting, the two ran from their pursuers.

The large hall was made of the slick marble structure which now lay in ruins after the attack. The two blurry children ran harder as they neared what appeared to be two round escape pods. Feet thudding on the ground, they narrowly made it into the pods. Both pods shot out through the broken sky and into the stars above.

"This is when we decided we had to take our accumulated knowledge and give it to another race to rebuild after the slaughter of our home world. But half way through our journey to your planet, we got separated. Thats why I...I..."

Kaiden was startled as everything suddenly snapped back to the present. The vision was gone, and the crying girl was frozen in place. With a sudden jerk, she shimmered and disappeared with a terrified look on her face.

"Wait!" Kaiden yelled to the now empty hallway. His hands shook as he got to his feet. How long had he been in the vision, and what happened to the crying girl?

"I have to tell Tera." He said, shaking off the weirdness of what had happened. They could figure this out. And maybe this is what those damn pills were suppressing. Maybe this war between the Aelores and Silores wasn't over. And just maybe he could help. He composed himself as he reached archives, then spotted a familiar face rushing out of the doors.

"Hey Tera. I really need to talk to you." He hissed under his breath, looking warily to the girl at Tera's side. With a slight asian girl in tow, both girls looked like they were ready to jump out of their skin from anxiety.

"This is a bad idea, Tera. Very, very bad idea. We could get into so much trouble." The small girl was saying frantically to the much taller one.

"Kaiden!" Tera exclaimed, finally seeing him approach. "Great! Lets talk in here!" Tera said, grabbing the him and the asian girl and pulling them back into a nearby closet.

"You guys, you have no idea about this discovery I just made!" Tera exclaimed in a raspy whisper.

"Excuse me, I was the one that pointed out to you," the small asian girl said.

"Tera, who is this?" Kaiden asked confused.

"Kaiden meet Yun. Yun meet Kaiden. She's new to archives. Yun is from child care." Tera said off handedly. Yun grinned and waved at Kaiden. Kaiden waved back awkwardly.

"This discovery we made. We found a file with the words, 'Project Beyond The Stars' and my…" Tera said, changing the topic.

"The crying girl she…" Kaiden spoke at the same time as Tera.

They were both cut off by loud pounding on

the metal closet door. All three of them jumped back with a yelp.

"60 seconds in heaven is over, you sicko love birds. Get your ugly butts out of there!" Came a familiar voice.

Kaiden opened the door to see Nora standing before them with twiddle dee and twiddle dumb in tow.

"Oh gross, there's three of you in there. I knew you were sick, but not that sick. You guys are so disgusting." She said, rolling her eyes as twiddle dee gave Kaiden a wink. He flushed uncomfortably.

"Oh, whatever Nora. Don't you have better things to do than harass me?" Tera asked, stepping up to the much taller girl.

Nora pretended to be bored by looking at her nails. "You really think this is all about you? Do you think this world revolves around you, Tera?" Nora asked, giving Tera flat look.

"We're here for your little midget friend over there. She has lab tests to do or something like that. Why those council lackeys send me, I will never know." Nora said, rolling her eyes pointing a lazy finger at Yun. All eyes turned to Yun.

Panting, Oscar slammed the door behind him. His lungs burned as his hands shook, more with excitement than age. Huffing, he slowly opened his hands to reveal the small feather. Its small glow of twinkling purple and blue strands made up of a hundred galaxies lay in his hands. The light was enough to illuminate his room. Sighing, he stroked the softness of the feather.

"Oh, Lily. They're still alive." He said with tears brimming his eyes as he slowly sunk to the floor, his back resting against the door.

"It has all been worth it. The sacrifices of so many lives are worth it just for this small token. This proof they survived." Slowly he got up, clutching the feather to his chest as he made his way across the room to turn on the one bulb in the middle of the room.

Sitting down at his desk, he gazed a photo of a much younger version of himself and a petite red headed woman. They were smiling in the picture. Oscar smiled to himself.

"*Lily*… Your sacrifice was the one to make this all possible." He spoke softly as he rested his head on the desk, and slowly drifted to another day.

A day a long time ago, a day with her. Her dazzling smile and auburn hair flowing as they swayed dancing in the kitchen. Lily laughed as she was spun about. Her laughter turned to screams mere seconds later as she slowly began to melt like a candle that was too hot in the oven. Lily's screams still echoed in his mind when he awoke in a cold sweat.

James Ward hummed to himself as he washed his hands. They were running out of surgical gloves, he would have to tell Tiffany about that. He watched as the water diluted the blood that ran from his hands and arms, turning it to a soft pink. It was almost beautiful today.

"Are you going to be much longer, Greg?" James called over his shoulder to the stout man who was mopping the floor. It was more actually like lazily pushing bloods and goo down the drain in the middle of the surgery room.

"Huh? Oh yeah boss, I'll be done real soon. I know you want to get out of here." Greg called back, pushing the mixture only slightly faster than he was before.

James had once been repulsed by the work he had been required to do, but they were running out of time. It seemed to be the only thing he could think about lately. Time. The sacrifices he saw were reduced to sheer butchery. But not all of the experiments ended this way. Some were success on a varying degree. James had yet to see a real, solid success though. One that would give him hope that there was still time left, and his mission could be accomplished. That success could possibly be in the form of Miss Yun Chang.

Yun waited anxiously. She had done the lab work before and survived where many other kids had not. She knew that for a fact. She sat bouncing her legs nervously as she waited on the cold bench in her waiting room with blank worn white walls. She hoped she could stay with her new friends. She liked Tera… she was funny and dramatic. Kaiden was kinda cute for someone who seemed a bit dark, even though he was a few years her senior.

To finally make friends that won't disappear on me like the ones I met in Childcare. That was a comforting thought, and she smiled to herself while looking down at her feet and pulling at her hair thoughtfully.

A knock sounded at the door. "Miss Chang?"

"Yes?" She called to the male voice.

The heavy door of the cramped waiting room clunked open, and a silver-haired man walked in wearing a lab coat over his colony jumpsuit. His smile was charming for a man his age, Yun thought.

"I am James Ward. You can just call me James." He said smoothly.

"Well, you already know my name because of the chart." She said, flushing, and gesturing awkwardly to the manilla folder in his hand.

"Thats right, Miss Chang, I sure do know an awful lot about you, and your time in child care as well." He said, his smile never wavering though his once-shimmering eyes now took on a almost dull, dead look.

"Tell me Miss Chang, have you had any increase of the side effects lately? It says here in your chart that you had began to see creatures that weren't there in the child care room." He said, taking a seat on a rolling stool next to her.

"It is reported here that you claimed those creatures you saw," he chuckled to himself, "were talking to you."

"Those... you want to talk about them?" She said, eyes tearing up and a lump increasing in her throat. She swallowed hard, looking at James.

"They haven't shown up since the new dosage of the pills." She stammered, as a flash of a memory from not too long ago bubbled up in her memory. The floor stained red with blood, and in her mind, a large feathered wolf stood before her. The feathers shimmered in a multitude of colors. She only called it a "*wolf*" because it was the closest thing she could describe it as from the pictures she had seen.

With the glimmer of a million stars. It stared down at her with piercing set of four indigo eyes, a dog-like snout and pointed ears, with six legs. "*Yun Chang*" it had echoed in her mind, so loud, as the blood of the others streamed like rivers between its massive paws.

"Tell me, have the Aelore spoken to you recently, Miss Chang?" He asked in a low growl of a whisper.

Tera and Kaiden sat on the floor of his dorm. They both sat with legs crossed and a single sheet of paper in between them, torn and battered with age.

"Tera, will you listen to me? Something happened earlier!" Kaiden said, almost frantically.

Tera was so consumed with these papers she found she wasn't hearing a word he said.

"Hmm…" she said, not paying attention.

Fed up with her antics, he leaned over to her and grabbed her chin, pulling her face into his.

He didn't expect being this close would feel like that, especially since they napped together almost every morning. They both flushed. A long dark curl had fallen into her face, and her light brown eyes shimmered with excitement over her research. Kaiden cleared his throat.

"The crying girl appeared to me during the day… I had a vision." Kaiden said.

"You what?" Tera said, dropping the piece of paper in her hand. He recounted the vision to her as best he could remember, not skipping anything.

Tera sat back, her paper long since forgotten. Kaiden sat there looking at her, waiting for any sort of reaction.

"So you think these visions and my dreams are from the Aelore? I thought they were extinct. From all the records, they should be." Tera said, looking up at the ceiling as if to see the answers to the mysteries up there.

"Or maybe it's all some weird side effect from not taking the pills." Kaiden said, leaning his head tiredly in his hand.

"If that's true, then why haven't I experienced anything?" Tera said musingly.

"What if she really is an Aelore, and you're

on some type of secret mission to save them?" Tera chuckled, seeing Kaiden's weak smile.

"Oh… Will I see you tonight?" Kaiden asked, reaching for her by instinct only.

"Yeah, the usual meeting spot?" She asked, allowing him to touch her arm.

Kaiden was awake, his earlier tiredness seemingly washed away. He lay in his bed, watching the semi-busted clock in his room. Any minute, she would come and cry, and there wasn't a damn thing he could to to stop it. Bored, he began to get dressed for the inevitable. Then, he could meet with Tera in their spot.

Pacing the room, he watched the clock. The crying girl was late. Surely the "vision" from earlier wasn't the same girl, or it was some sort of crazy side effect. That's what he finally told himself: she was late. She should have shown up by now.

He began to pace, muttering to himself.

"I don't get it. Where is she…? She has never been late."

That's when he heard it.

The crying.

He was almost so overwhelmed with the joy of her appearance that he could have hugged the starry little specter, but then he noticed that something was off...

She appeared as normal, standing crying softly to herself in the corner. But there was another shape behind her, a new one... This one was much taller. It was hard to make out in the dark, but it looked similar to the being from the earlier vision. The Silore.

"Hey, get away from her!" Kaiden yelled, defensively.

The new being had two pin pricks of light where the eyes should be, but there was not much else to it. It seemed to be blacker than the deepest shadows of the room. It turned its dark, smoky head towards him.

"*She is ours...*" It said in a thousand resounding voices of different ages and pitches. The crying girl let out one scream that seemed to shake the whole room, and they were gone.

CHAPTER
4

The dreams always started out the same way. Tera was now standing in the mosaic hallway. The two golden doors from her last dream now were closed behind her.

The hallway was the same almost iridescent marble, though to her right were large carved archways which boasted a magnificent view of the planets and distant stars. The hall was chilly, and the room was noiseless, except for a muffled sound that came from the end of the hall. Steeling herself, and against her better judgment, Tera continued forward, keeping one hand on the slick wall of the hallway.

"These dreams are really getting out of hand." She muttered to herself. Out one of the last windows, she could see a distant planet with two oddly colored moons.

"I don't think we're on Earth anymore." She said to herself, as she paused to take in the scene before her.

"That almost looks like what Kaiden described from his visitation from the crying girl." She said under her breathe in awe.

"What were those pills really dampening?" She wondered.

"I guess I'll just have to find out for myself." Tera thought, as she continued down the hall.

She stood before two doors. They were massive and made up of the same shimmery gold-type material as the other door in the first room, with the same complex designs decorating them. As she neared the doors, one of them popped open with a loud whoosh. She could feel the change of pressure as the door slowly slid open. Tendrils of mist lazily crept out of the small opening in the doorway. She could hear muffled crying coming from inside the room.

"Not weird at all. Lets go into the strange room, Tera. Great idea." She said to herself, as she gently pushed open the door. Inching her way in, she realized the large room was made entirely of gold.

In the farthest end of the room sat what appeared to be a young boy, dressed in lavish and luxurious clothing. The garments were deep in color and meticulous designs constructed of gold. It made Tera's own jumpsuit look like a dirty rag in comparison.

The small being was wiping its eyes as she entered.

"Tera Ward. Greetings, I am The Eternal Loirail of the Aelore." The child king's voice resounded in Tera's mind. The Loirial sat still, boring into her soul with mismatched indigo and amethyst eyes. He seemed to be waiting for something.

Tera's jaw dropped in shock. It was the same. The same as Kaiden's vision, except she was seeing the male counterpart. Her feet began to move on their own, as if drawn to the child king. She made it up to the steps of the dais in a few seconds. It was a dream after all, so she could probably fly if she wanted to. She would have to try that later, Tera mused to herself.

"My sister told me that she has made contact with your companion, Kaiden Lewis." The Loriail said, looking down at her from his throne.

"My what? Kaiden isn't my *companion*. He's just a good friend." She said, taken aback from the dream's words.

The Loirial stared, considering her, for a moment, then finally spoke *"No matter. Kaiden also has received the information we wanted to send you."* The Loirial said.

"But I have one message, for you." The Loriail said, raising from the dais. It strode toward her with long flowing hair that draped like a long curtain over the dais. It shimmered with an almost glow. The skin of the child king was pale, but as it got closer, she saw that it appeared to be made up with of millions of stars, so close together that they gave the appearance of being pale.

It continued to stare at Tera as it stood a few steps above her.

"You and I. We are the same." It said, as it took the last few steps down until it was eye level with her. Gingerly, it reached out a hand and touched her forehead. She felt a lighting bolt of energy slam into her mind. She felt herself fall, and everything faded to black.

"Save us, Tera." She heard a voice whisper as her eyes shot open. Her body was covered in sweat, and her stomach twisted. There was a new emotion: fear.

"How can I be the same as that kid?" She muttered to herself as she got out of bed. Kaiden would definitely want to hear about this.

Nora couldn't sleep, which was unusual for

her, since she had always prided herself on her beauty sleep. She had read somewhere that a woman's worth was only skin deep. She saw that had some use to her.

If she could fool people into giving her what she wanted because of her beauty, who was she to complain? It only made getting her way that much easier.

This night though, she chose to blame her random case of unexplained insomnia on that stupid note she found telling her not to take the pills. So, rising to the challenge, she did as it instructed.

Stretching, she got up from the bed and made her way to the bathroom. She splashed her face with the slightly murky-looking water, and ran her damp hands through her long blonde hair. Her complexion was clear for the most part, except for a smattering of a few random freckles, which must have appeared when she was younger.

A time that she couldn't remember. A time when they lived on the surface and saw the sun. She always wondered who she was back then, and what was it like to run in the sunshine without a care in the world.

She was tall for her age, but as far as puberty went, that was about it. She was a gangly, flat thing. Oh sure, her friends said she was slender and graceful like a swan. She had seen pictures of swans, and she certainly didn't feel like one. She felt more like an ostrich with gangly long stick legs. She towered over some of the boys in the colony. Which made her feel like a giant…

Her stomach twisted as a memory of a cute boy would run up to her ask her how the weather was, and take off running, only to laugh about it with his friends. That had happened too often to her in childcare years ago.

More memories began to flood her brain. They started slow, one little memory at a time. The memories would come in a flash of images, until they blurred together, and then would snap, focusing on just one image.

The image floating in her mind was a picture of four people. A man and woman, both fair of features. The woman had dark blonde hair, and the man still had light blonde hair. Between them were two children: one was a 7 year old boy with dark blonde hair, and the other was a little girl about 5 years old with almost white blonde hair and a light dusting of freckles across her cheeks..

"What in the world?" Nora breathed through a flurry of rapid heartbeats, her stomach twisting further. The image began to pop, and it soon melted away, revealing a image of the galaxy. Hundreds of thousands of stars shown brightly.

This was strange for Nora, as she could still feel the cold bathroom floor. Even so, she felt like she was *in* space.

"Nora Martin, I can lend you my powers in exchange for your memories." The voice resounded through her brain.

"My memories?" She whispered, feeling a small trickle of blood drip from her nose.

"I can lend you my powers to aid you." The voice said.

Nora paused for a moment.

"Is this freaky stuff what those pills were keeping back?" She wondered to herself.

Most importantly, she could remember life before this place and her family. She had a brother. She assumed she had parents, but never guessed she had siblings. Maybe he survived.

"I'll do it, Random Voice In This Bad Case Of Insomnia." She said in her mind. She could feel the whatever it was smiling back somehow in the vision.

"Excellent." It said, as she began to feel hot, like her limbs were on fire. She clenched her teeth and let out a scream. Her whole world was set

ablaze, all went dark.

The bathroom door burst open, with a loud boom.

"Hey… Hold on Nora… Hold on!" A voice said.

Nora's eyes were blurry. Her skin felt cooler. She sat up with the aid of someone.

"Easy does it." Said the voice.

Blinking away the final blurriness of her vision, she turned to see, Tera Ward, helping her up, with about the biggest look of concern on her face. What a dork.

"Are you okay? I heard an explosion, and found you here, untouched." Tera said.

The bathroom lay in blackened rubble.

The mirror was all but melted. Panicked, Nora looked down at herself. There was nothing on her. No dirt. No soot. What had happened? Powers. That vision thing gave her powers.

"What was going on in this place?" Nora wondered to herself.

"Well, this has all been really weird, but I am glad you're okay." Tera said, slowly backing away from Nora, almost as if she was afraid of her.

Then Nora looked down at her hands. As she moved her fingers, they glittered slightly in the now-dimming bathroom light. That was weird... maybe it was part of those powers. She actually felt much better than earlier.

"Well then, freak. You don't look so grand, yourself." Nora said with a smirk, as she pointed to Tera's hair.

"Where'd you find the bleach? Or did you just want to be so much like me that you would do something that looked so awful?" She laughed at Tera.

Tera flushed, having not the slightest clue what Nora was talking about or why she was being such jerk. Then Tera saw it as the last piece of the bathroom mirror began to fall. Her once raven black hair was now white as snow. Actually, it was lighter than Nora's now, and seemed to glimmer of a light all of its own.

"You and I are the same." The child king's words echoed in her head.

"Well, thats great, think what you want, glitter jazz hands. I really must find Kaiden." Tera said, wiggling her fingers in front of Nora's face.

"Oh, and you're welcome for the help." Tera

said storming out, panic rising in her chest. How had Kaiden changed, if any, from seeing the crying girl?

"Kaiden? What's going on with Kaiden?" Nora called after Tera as she fled the room. Nora wiggled her hands she watched the shimmery light move just under her skin, reacting to the movement.

"Weird powers, huh. Let's see what we can do, then." She said to the empty bathroom. Determined to help Kaiden, she bolted out of the room following the sounds of Tera's footsteps. She most certainly wasn't doing this to repay that freak Tera.

Kaiden paced back and forth. It seemed to him that today was the day that everyone was late, he mused to himself. The trash collection area was one of the few places that people wouldn't dare to venture. It was smelly, but it was good enough for them. Everywhere else was heavily guarded by personnel and orderlies. Though many of them weren't much older than Kaiden himself, it was thought to be an honored position among the children. No more cataloging of dead men's thoughts and other such boring menial tasks.

"The crying girl." He thought, looking up at

the ceiling.

"Where did she go? What did the Silore mean when it said she was theirs? Or did it kill her?" Kaiden didn't know the answers to any of these questions.

Though the girl had been a nuisance for a while now, he had started to like the nightly routine, if for no other reason than to spend time with Tera, exchanging stories and theories of what they thought it all meant.

It worried him that Tera was late, that the crying girl disappeared with one of those Silores. All things that were out of his control, and that frustrated him to no end.

Heavy foot falls sounded to his right.

"Tera you took forever. I have things I need to tell you. The crying girl, she…" he stopped mid-sentence as two large men dressed in white jumpsuits approached him.

"The crying girl, you say? Funny, you didn't mention her in today's session, Kaiden…" A familiar voice said from behind the two men.

James Ward stood in front of Kaiden, hands clasped behind his back, with a keen look in his eyes. James was nearly as tall as the two bruisers.

"Yes, in fact, it's not recorded anywhere in your files. But that will be discussed later." James said, almost mockingly.

Kaiden glared. This was the man responsible for everything. Kaiden knew it deep down in his gut. The two other men didn't wait for Kaiden to respond, and grabbed him roughly by the arms, dragging him. Kaiden thrashed, resisting the orderlies but their grips were to strong.

"What are you doing, James? " Kaiden bellowed, twisting to see James.

"I need you for questioning." James said, as he thrust a black sack over Kaiden's head. Kaiden's cries and protests were muffled under the sack.

A pen clicked three times. Tera could hear it as she stood silently against the wall of the dorms. Something was definitely going on here. What was Amy Gomez doing here in the dorms and blocking Tera's exit to see Kaiden?

"Miss Ward… I haven't got all night to play this little game. So if you would come out nicely, that would be great. You too, Miss Martin." Amy Gomez said, as she looked down at her chart clicking her pen only twice.

"Miss Martin?!" Tera thought, then she looked behind her. There stood that giant with sparkling hands in the dark, a few dozen paces behind her. Stupid, Tera. She met eyes with Nora, who waved a little guiltily.

"We have to surrender, Tera." Nora said, through gritted teeth.

"Use your jazz hands, Nora!" Tera whispered, frantically.

"I have no idea how to do that, Tera. Until I can figure it out, we have to play along." Nora said, as she shoved past

Tera entered the hallway. Accompanying Amy were two burly looking women dressed in white jump suits. Orderlies. "Great." Tera thought to herself.

"Now that's a nice girl. Miss Martin, would you kindly bring out your little friend so we can get on with this? The council doesn't take lightly to girls who clearly lie to us. " Amy said with a tired but frank expression.

Tera looked on as burly woman number one grabbed Nora roughly by the arm and put a sack over her head.

"There's no way out of this one," Tera

thought to herself, as she slowly stepped out from her hiding spot.

"There we are. What a good girl." Amy said, in a sarcastic cooing voice, clicking her pen three times and jotting something on her clip board.

Tera grunted as burly woman number two roughly shoved the sack over her own head. It wasn't until this moment in total darkness of the hood she thought back to her dream. She had been so busy dealing with Nora's own issues that the dream had almost slipped from her grasp.

She couldn't forget what the child king had said. And what happened to Nora only made everything else so much more important. They were clearly getting messages from an alien race that, as far as they knew, had gone extinct in *The Great War.*

Yun didn't know why she was still in Questioning, but what she did know was that if she pretended to be unconscious, the questions stopped. And, that she was in a small cell with rusted metal bars to keep her from leaving.

Yun heard the door slam open, accompanied by muffled cries of protest. She dared to peak through her eyelashes. She could make out that figures entering the room; two were dressed in white with a colonist in tow with a black sack over their head. The other figure was clearly James.

None of the kids forgot him. She could still feel his creepy aura on her as he asked her question after question about what happened in child care, and the wolves.

What happened that day to the children?

Blood. There had been so much blood. And the creature in the corner of the room made up of smokey stars staring back at her while the feathered wolf stood between her and the creature. She couldn't save them, and still didn't know why she was spared. She had cried for the wolf to save the other children, but it didn't seem to hear her, and only stood by as a silent sentinel.

James tore off the sack off of Kaiden's head. Kaiden spit at him, and James returned the favor with a square punch to the jaw.

"Put him over there with Miss Chang. She's so drugged up, it wont bother her." James said, gesturing to her cell.

The two orderlies opened the door and easily tossed Kaiden in the cell with her. He landed on the ground with a grunt. Kaiden swore fluently at the three men.

Yun sat up when she could sense the coast was clear.

"Hey stranger!" Yun said, tapping him on the shoulder. Kaiden jumped back in surprise

"Yun! I thought they drugged you?" Kaiden said in a hushed whisper, looking towards the door through which James and the orderlies had left.

"They thought they did. We all know how easy it is to fake the effects of the drugs." she said proudly and grinned at him keenly, dimples appearing on both sides of her cheeks.

"They asked a lot of questions, but one of them I still can't figure out." Yun said absently, staring off into the distance.

"Did you and Tera figure out what was up with that file?" she said, leaning in excitedly changing the topic from her personal pain.

Kaiden ran his hair through his even messier mop of hair.

"No. Unfortunately, we talked about other things and completely spaced the files." He said, looking at the small girl next to him. He stared intently into her dark eyes, then took her by the shoulders.

"Yun, there are things going on here. Things that are getting weirder. I don't want something bad to happen to you. A lot of the things I can't explain. No one can. But maybe there are answers in the files that Tera has. We need to get out of here and find her." He said, relaxing his grip.

Her excitement waned, and almost disappeared. Despite her feelings, Yun held onto her cheerful attitude, seeing how Kaiden really needed some hope right now. The worry was all over his handsome face. Which worried her.

"Someone is coming!" Yun said, pulling Kaiden.

The creature was waiting for Oscar. It always waited for him. It would kill him one of these days, and Oscar knew it. Was today that day? Or would he live a little longer to somehow atone for his crimes; crimes that still haunted Oscar's waking and sleeping moments. Oscar began to wonder if he truly deserved to be here in Lily's stead. He had tried to be cleansed of his sins. To erase all of this horrific mess.

Oscar stared at the creature in the darkness

of his room. Its six eyes shone like the brightest, stars, staring at him, unfeeling.

"Will today be the day you get me?" Oscar croaked, as he stood up from the desk where he had fallen asleep.

He tucked the photo of he and Lily into his back pocket. Today was the day. He was going to choose his destiny. His only hope was that Tera and the others had heeded his warning. He hoped he was not too late. Clutching the feather in his hand as if it gave him strength, Oscar ran. And there was nothing the Silore could do to stop him.

CHAPTER 5

Tera's world was dark. With her vision blocked, she could feel every rock and bump in the floor as her body was dragged like a animal to the slaughter. She could barely make out Nora's whimpers and pleas to be let go. Tera wished for once that Nora would shut her big mouth. After all, it was Nora's fault they were in this situation. If Nora couldn't figure out how to use those jazz hands for destruction, they were done for.

Through her hood, she could hear muffled speech and feel the change in air pressure, and a slam of a door. They had changed rooms apparently, and were no longer in the hallway. What kept nagging at the back of her head was that she wasn't able to meet up with Kaiden yet to tell him her recent discoveries. And tell him about Nora's new abilities, if they could be called that.

A clank and the squeal of rusted metal grinding against rusted metal, and then the beefy hands of her captor tossed her like she weighed no more than a sack of potatoes.

"Oof!" Tera cried, as she landed hard. She

could feel grit and dirt and rocks beneath her.

"Why don't you two cool off with your little friends." Amy called out. "James will be out soon, he's just tying up loose ends."

Small hands untied the hood, and pulled it off of her head. Tera blinked her eyes against the bright light of the cell.

"Here you go... almost good as new," a gentle voice said. When her vision cleared, Tera could see Yun in front of her, and Kaiden taking off Nora's hood.

Blood was running from Tera's head, and she saw Nora wince at her arm being touched. The four of them huddled together, Tera reached out and hugged Yun tightly.

"Yun, I am so glad you're okay! I was so worried." She exclaimed sympathetically.

"What on Earth are you doing here?" Kaiden asked Nora, who's haughty expression had returned, replacing the emotional state Tera had seen earlier.

"Me? Pshha! I got caught up in this mess with your freak of a friend over there. All I wanted to do was use the freakin' bathroom." Nora scoffed, rolling her eyes and holding her injured arm.

"Excuse me! You were the one who sold me out to Amy. I was just trying to meet Kaiden at our meeting spot and you got in the way." Tera exclaimed at the other girl.

"You what?!" Yun and Nora squealed in disgusted horror.

"You, meet with Kaiden alone? In the middle of the night. For what? A hook up?!" Yun scoffed, face turning red.

"How dare you! You harlot! Kaiden is far too handsome for the likes of you!" Nora screeched, almost cradling Kaiden with her good arm.

"A hook up? What no, its not like that?! We discuss things." Tera said defensively.

"Oh, give me a break! I'm sure you have real, in-depth discussions at weird hours of the night." Nora said, a sarcastic kissy face.

"Ladies! Ladies, settle down. What Tera says is true. We talk about the weird things that are going on in the colony. The dreams and visions that we experience at night. That is all." Kaiden said, putting his hands up in a defensive position, avoiding the glares from Nora and Yun.

"That's pretty flimsy, but whatever..." Nora said, wincing as she tried to cross her arms.

"Well, what do you guys think it means? I mean, that is what James asked me about…" Yun said, not making eye contact. "Your dad is like, super creepy, Tera…"

Tera looked away nervously, as her own memories of James came flooding back. James softly humming a tuneless melody, with blood and the glitter of starlight swirling around the room.

"I know he is," Tera said, softly.

"That's beside the point though, Kaiden." Tera said, ignoring the other two girls and staring her friend in the eyes. He had to know. Something was happening. Maybe that's what the visions were: to warn them. Or doom them.

"Oh, by the way, I like your new hair?" Yun asked, concerned.

"Well, thats different, Tera." Kaiden said, only now noticing the change. "And whats up with your hands, Nora?"

"Well, you see, that's what I have been trying to tell you abo…" Tera was abruptly cut off by the door crashing open with a loud boom.

Tobias would not have been considered a brilliant man by any stretch of the imagination, but he was strong and he minded his own business. That's how the council liked it. He could handle the farming tools just fine. He would finish his work far sooner than many of the other farmhands would. He was 14 when we was recruited from the All Saints Orphanage For Troubled Boys And Girls in downtown L.A. Or from what other people had said, what used to be downtown L.A.; most of the buildings were leveled in the attacks 8 years ago.

The woman who had recruited him was a hispanic woman that could easily have looked like what his mother might have looked like if she had survived the attacks. But so few of the adults had. Disease and mysterious disappearances were rampant at that time. The orphanage had been run by older kids that the council had deemed loyal enough.

But, that was a long time ago. Much of the rubble had been cleared to make way for farming or for some sort of council agency. Tobias didn't know much about that. And he didn't care to. He just swung the hoe. A few boys from the orphanage were still here, though many of them didn't talk to each other. It wasn't that they couldn't, so much as it had been what they had seen. There are some things a person can't forget, and would rather not speak about. That was their quiet way on the colony farm.

The sky was alight with a multitude of colors; from the setting sun. He liked the colors, they were always different, and he liked that… something that wasn't always the same. Change was good in a simple life like his. A little was enough for him.

A freckle faced, red headed man a few years his senior came up to Tobias.

"Did 'ja finish early again?" Jerry said with an accent, huffing only slightly from his jaunt from the barn.

"Sure did." Tobias said. As Tobias walked past Jerry, he suddenly grabbed Tobias' arm. Tobias jumped in surprise.

"The woman. She's here." Jerry said with panic in his eyes.

Tobias had nothing to say to that, but just nodded. The woman. Tobias shuddered. She was a cruel woman. Again, he wasn't a smart man, but felt compassion for his terrified companion.

"I'll see what she wants." He said with a flat expression.

Amy Gomez waited impatiently, tapping her

foot. She had changed from her colony clothes into a nice pencil skirt, button top, and heels. She had to keep the appearances up for the people on the surface. Something she didn't have to do down in the colony. She swore under her breath as she smoothed out the tight bun of her hair. If it wasn't for those few hooligans, she wouldn't have to do this.

After the flood of a few years back, started by some wise cracks who thought they could wipe out the whole colony with a flood. Those individuals had paid the ultimate price for their little failed experiment.

"It doesn't matter now. All that matters right now is that we handle the entrance to the farm. Which any idiot could handle." Amy said to herself, as she self consciously smoothed the wrinkles out of her skirt again waiting for Tobias.

What Tera Ward and her little friend Kaiden Lewis didn't know was that their little nightly hide out was dangerously close to the grate that lead to the farm. To the surface. Imagine that! How would a dolt like Tobias react to kids emerging from the drains? He would lose it for sure. Or find the truth and revolt. They all might revolt against the colony's control.

That would never happen, she reassured herself. Tobias was a man of no great position at the farm, but he was loyal and too stupid to think for himself, which helped them in this case. She turned as Tobias entered the room, wearing dirty and worn overalls. His skin was dark and dirty from laboring outside in the sun.

"Miss Gomez?" Tobias said, taking his worn baseball cap off of his head. His dark hair was matted from sweat. He looked at her with the earnest eyes of a doe in the scope of a hunter.

"We've been having some complications in the colony. You haven't seen or heard anything strange? Especially coming from this grate?" Amy said, tapping the toe of one heeled shoe on the large grate which they used to deliver food as well as dispose of trash.

It was also a way for privileged personnel like herself to go to the surface for other business when called for.

Tobias' eyes drifted down to the grate in the floor, knowing that he and the other hands had been hearing strange things for months from the grate. Some of the men, usually the younger ones, thought it was monsters of some sort, and older men said it was some type of military training ground.

Tobias thought it was neither. He had heard another man whispering to someone a few days back, but he couldn't tell if it was real or not... or the same voices that were always talking to him.

Sometimes they even came in a more physical form. But always at night. They almost blended into the night. They were so dark. Tobias wasn't a smart man, but he knew there was something wrong going on down there.

"*Lie.*" Said a small crackling voice in his head.

"No ma'am. Me and Jerry, we do our rounds and nothing new happens... its always the same." Tobias said, giving Amy an innocent look.

"That's good enough, Tobias." She said curtly, smoothing out her skirt again. Would it kill James to allow them a simple iron? She clicked her pen three times.

Oscar rushed into the room with the Silore gaining on his heels. Oscar looked around the room frantically until he spotted Tera and a few other kids from the colony in a barred cell.

"Oscar! What are you doing here?" Tera exclaimed, in confusion.

"Tera! Thank goodness you aren't harmed!." Oscar said, dashing towards the cell.

"I don't have a lot of time left. Know that all of this I am doing for you." Oscar said with tears in his eyes, and a smile that radiated love.

A mocking applause began from the new figure in the room.

"I am so glad you could make time for our little pow-wow, Oscar." James said, smiling wickedly.

Oscar turned to James, standing and facing him.

"I am here to fulfill my end of the bargain, James." Oscar said, as the Silore had slithered into the room, shifting from shadow to shadow. Tera gasped.

"Oscar! What are you doing with a Silore?!" Tera said in shock.

"Who cares! As long as it leaves us alone, I am okay with that!" Nora exclaimed.

Yun huddled in the back, whispering things to the empty air next to her. Kaiden stood, heart racing.

"If it gets in here, we are done for!" Kaiden said, trying his best to sound brave.

The hulking beast nearly hit the ceiling. It hissed as it turned its head towards James.

"A Silore? How original. Old man, I didn't

know you still had those connections to the council." James said, gritting his teeth.

"This?" Oscar motioned to the beast.

"This contract was one I made a long time ago, son. One that my Lily paid for in the worst way. But it doesn't matter, today is the day I atone for that sin. Atone for all of this wrong and evil I brought to the colony, with the help of you, James. These injustices end today." Oscar said smugly.

"You don't understand what you just did, you old fool! By bringing *it* here." James cursed and looked terrified at the same time.

"Oh, I know exactly what I've done. I have sealed your fate, and mine, this day." Oscar said, as he pulled the galaxy feather from his pocket, pointing it like a weapon towards James. James looked at the feather in shock.

"Where did you get that? They died in the war. They all did. I was the last." James said in astonishment.

"The last Aelore left on earth." James said, falling to his knees, tears streaming down his face, looking at the feather as if it was the most precious thing on Earth.

Oscar released his grip on the feather. As it slowly drifted into James's hands, the Silore made its move. With a loud screech, it was on James in two bounds. James screamed as the creature tore its claw-like hands through his chest. James's skin began to bubble and fall away like peeling paint. Under his flesh appeared to be not muscle, but stars. Millions of stars that encompassed his dark form. His eyes turned indigo and amethyst.

"I did it. I saved them." James muttered in a voice that echoed through the room, as his body began to shine brighter and brighter until it suddenly blinked out.

The Silore cackled to itself as it cocked its head towards the group in the cell. Oscar wiped a tear away, and turned towards the Silore.

"No! That's not our arrangement. I was to give you James and I have. Now uphold your end, and leave those kids alone." Oscar said, as he stood defiantly between the Silore and the cell. The Silore regarded him thoughtfully.

""True, the half-breeds from James were not a part of our original agreement. Perhaps you would like to reconsider?" The Silore echoed. Oscar shook his head.

"Never! Fulfill your end of the bargain, monster." Oscar said, holding his hands out wide.

The Silore almost gleefully strode over to Oscar and ran him through the chest. Oscar grunted and slumped to the ground as the Silore disappeared like mist in the shining sun.

"Nora do something! He's dying!" Tera screamed.

Nora's hands began to shake. Panicked, Nora reached out to the bars and grabbed them into her hands.

"I don't know if this will work, Tera. But I'll try." Nora cried out, as the other three looked on.

She focused her thoughts onto the bars. Slowly, inside of her, she could see a pin pick of light. The rusted metal bars in Nora's hands got hot. They began to glow a bright orange and bubble into liquid, hissing as it splattered on the ground.

With a few of the bars melted away, Tera squeezed through them. She stumbled her way to Oscar. Dark blood had begun to stain the ground.

"Oscar! Oscar!" Tera cried out, her hands shaking and heart racing in her chest, as she wrapped one arm around his torso trying to slow the bleeding. Her other hand cradled his hands. Coughing, he gave Tera a weak smile.

"It's okay, Tera. It was supposed to be this way." He said, gently taking her hand in his.

Behind her, Tera could hear Yun begin to cry

softly. Nora and Kaiden stood back awkwardly, sobbing as Oscar took his last breath. Tera gasped wide eyed to find a note written in a cramped shaky lettering in her palm.

"Oh Oscar, what did you do." She whispered, as tears streamed down her face.

"Today ends my contract with the Silores. Colony will be in danger with James gone. Find the delivery shaft and the farm. Tobias will help you."-Oscar Ward

CHAPTER
6

"So, I guess we have to go the the surface."
Tera said, looking around at the small group before her. Kaiden, Nora, Yun, and herself had fled the Labs not long after Tera had found the note.

They had decided to regroup near the dorms. The had packed what little belongings they had. Tera's eyes were still puffy from lack of sleep and crying. The others didn't look like they were in much better shape.

Tera at least had enough time to wash her face and hands. Her hands, which had been covered in Oscar's blood. She wouldn't even let herself think about James, let alone process it, until they were somewhere safer. The colony obviously was no longer a safe place for them. The sirens had stared blaring every few minutes after they left the Labs; one of the orderlies must have pulled the alarm.

The halls were lit up with red flashing lights and a loud obnoxious noise. The alarms hadn't sounded for almost as long as Tera could remember, and it had thrown the rest of the colony into chaos. Tera figured that was a good thing. Maybe they could get lost in the masses and make their escape.

"We really should get going soon. The longer we wait here, the sooner the orderlies will find us." Kaiden said stiffly.

He had blamed himself for not being able to help back in the Lab. He should have been able to do something. He hated being useless. The three girls looked at him, each nodding slowly.

"I know we are all scared right now. But with what we witnessed, we are going to be in a lot of trouble."

BLAAAAAAAAARROOOO

The alarms howled overhead as the pounding of rushing orderlies ran past them with flashlights, infesting the dorms like a hive of ants at a picnic.

Silently, the small group jogged down the now empty hallway as the alarms faded into the background.

Tera felt like she was in a dream. Her body felt numb, like it was happening to someone else. As she followed close behind Kaiden and the other two behind her, Tera was glad to let him take the lead. She was so tired of being the leader. And right now, she honestly just wanted to lay in her bed and cry. Tears welled up and her throat tightened.

"No, I cant think about all of that. The others need me to be strong. I may not have powers like Nora, but I can be strong in my own way." Blinking away tears, she ducked into a dark alcove with the rest of them, letting another group of orderlies scurry past them.

Her heart pounded in her chest as she tried to keep her breathing as shallow as possible. Without warning, one of the orderlies stopped in front of their hiding place, calling out to his companions. A cold sweat ran down Tera's back as the man looked Tera straight in the face. Thankful for the safety of the darkness of the alcove, she remained motionless, even knowing that they had to keep moving. The farm and Tobias weighed on Tera's mind. She needed answers. The wait seemed like forever, but finally the man moved on. They all breathed a collective sigh of relief.

"That was a close one." Yun said softly.

Kaiden looked down both sides of the hallway, and motioned the girls to follow him. As they left the safety of the alcove, a shadow began to separate itself from the darkness, gathering other shadows around it as it began to darken the entire hallway behind them. The shadows formed into three large dark beings with seemingly too many arms.

Owen Benson hated bad news. As he poured over Amy Gomez's report, he sighed. This was just not his day, he decided. Or night, rather. The destruction of the rest of the council members was actually the best thing for his stress levels in decades. If the world ever got back on its feet, he would write a self-help book about it one day.

"How To Solve Your Stress With Murder." He laughed at his own joke.

"Is something funny, Owen? This is really, really bad." Amy said, as she paced, her heels clicking on the floor.

She didn't have time to change back. Since they were the council, there was no reason to wear these awful heels. Her feet ached, and she was tired. Her trip to the farm had gone smoothly enough, but when she got back, she discovered the near destruction of the colony. James and Oscar dead. Everything else was in chaos.

"I didn't know what to do, Owen. We don't have protocol for this. We had no idea about

James." Amy said, clicking her pen three times and holding her clipboard as if it was a pillow.

She stared at Owen tiredly, her feet protesting with each step. Owen looked like he was just back from a nice vacation with that smug smile on his face. He was an insufferable man most of the time, but right now, he was extra irritating. Owen sat back in his chair.

"It's simple, Amy. Burn down the farm and destroy the colony." Owen said, with a devious smile that could rival the devil's.

"What? You can't be serious. That would kill hundreds people and destroy valuable resources. Not to mention 8 years worth of research. Even if James was an Aelore, his research is priceless." Amy said defensively.

"He's lost his mind." Amy thought to herself.

"Yes, what you don't seem to grasp right now is that we are in it deep. Silores will not take kindly to us when they find out what James was. And they experiments he was running." Owen said, leaning over his desk, shoving a file in front of Amy. It read; "CONFIDENTIAL."

The folder itself was worn with age and damage. The first page read "Project Beyond the Stars. Oscar Ward and James Ward."

Amy gave Owen a flat look. "This project failed. Everyone knows that."

"And what if one of this program's founders was an Aelore in disguise? What then? That would compromise the whole operation. Maybe it failed because it didn't help the Silores, but the aided the Aelores instead." Owen said, rising from his chair.

"*If* James' experiments worked, Amy, it's worse than having Aelores, reproducing. James may have created a hybrid between humans and Aelores." He said, pacing the room.

The shadows in the room began to lengthen. The darkness seemed to swallow up what little light there had been in the room.

"They're here," Amy thought to herself, as a chill ran up her spine.

Owen ran his hands through his silver hair as he paced the room more frantically, and seemed to not notice the shadows. Those things, as vile as they were, actually helped mankind when it was on the brink of self destruction. Still, Silores had humanity chained like slaves.

The floor beneath them creaked as the Silores became more solid. There were rumors that they always existed in the shadows, waiting for their time to strike. But that was foolish.

"The Aelores have returned. What did you know about James' secret?" One of the the five Silores echoed, as they stood surrounding Amy and Owen.

Owen cleared his throat nervously.

"It's news to us. We had no idea that *thing* even existed. How could we? I didn't know that the Aelores could do such a thing. Besides, they were brought to extinction, by your reports." Owen said, feigning an air of indignation with the beasts.

The Silore that had spoken now stood mere inches away from Owen's face.

"We have our soldiers taking care of your mess, Owen. Don't let this happen again. The base will be destroyed, along with James' experiments." The Silore seemed to hiss as they disappeared.

Amy clicked her pen three times as the Silores evaporated like mist.

And just like that, they accepted the death sentence of all those who lived in the Colonies. It had to be done, she told herself.

Although the three dark forms stood behind the small group of humans, that wasn't what alerted Tera and her friends to their presence. It was the screams. Blood curdling screams filled the hallway on both sides.

"What in the world is going on?" Yun said, trembling.

"More importantly, what are those things doing here!" Nora exclaimed, as she stared opened-mouth at the three Silores that stood behind them.

"We are here to wipe out this infestation, half-breed." The Silore spoke into their minds, in a growl like chewing glass.

The other two Silore' lunged at the small group of people.

"RUN!" Kaiden yelled, as he sprinted towards the end of the hall, peeking only to see the others following as fast as they could. If they could just get to the grate. The surface had to be safe, right?

Screams echoed in the halls as they ran. The Silores were slaughtering colonists and orderlies alike, leaving no one alive.

They had to survive. Somehow they had to

fight the Silores. Tera balled her hands into fists, frustrated at her perceived lack of usefulness in this. The only person that had any sort of powers was Nora, and that was still really iffy. She had no plan and no real idea where the grate was. Her lungs burned and her legs ached with fatigue, but she kept running. All of them kept running.

Tera looked over at Kaiden. His face was determined, but, she could see a fear, not unlike hers. He was also doubting.

"You and I are one." The child king's words came back to her once more. If she and the child king shared powers or whatever, then what good was it doing now? In the vision Kaiden had, they had all ran. History was repeating itself. The Aelores would lose again.

Growling to herself with frustration and exhaustion, she thought maybe running wasn't the answer. Maybe they needed to fight. She would fight. There wasn't time to discuss, only, action now.

She stopped running and turned to face the oncoming Silores. They were huge. Almost as tall as the hall, and menacing in every definition of the word. They seemed to consume the light, though they glittered faintly with pin pricks of light, like a dying galaxy.

The others stopped a short distance ahead of

where Tera stood.

"Hey, what are you doing? Do you want to be killed?" Nora yelled, as she gasped for breath.

"I will fight these monsters, Nora. I'd rather die than let history repeat itself. And I am tired of running from everything." Tera said, feeling a sense of bravery and anger that she hadn't felt before.

A new-found rage seemed to spark something inside of her; like a raging wild fire, it seemed to consume her. She felt her head lower in determination. Her vision filled with the three Silores before her. She was tired. Tired of the death and destruction. Tired of losing.

She thought to herself. "Who's thoughts were these."

"*You and I are one.*" The voice of the child king filled her head again.

"Lend me your strength, and I will fight with you." She whispered to herself, feeling as if she wasn't alone, like somehow the child king was with her, standing with her, ready for the battle ahead. With a grin of confidence, she charged as she felt her body swell with light and power that replaced the burning rage.

It was hard to describe. She felt weightless, but ten times stronger than an entire army of Silores. Laughing to herself, she jumped. She flew feet off the ground, coming eye to eye with the six eyed aliens.

"This is for Earth." She whispered, as she felt the energy inside of her boil out and explode in a sea of light and white fire.

Her body seemed to turn into a large nebula. And with that flash, the Silores hissed, and then nothing was left of them. Just ash.

Tera felt her body slowly float down, and gently collapse on the floor of the hallway.

"That. Was. AMAZING!" Yun screamed with joy. Tears streamed down her face as she ran into a flying leap of a hug onto Tera.

"And here I thought what I could do was cool." Nora said, amazed for once.

Kaiden stared wide eyed.

"What did you do?" He asked, concerned.

"I don't really know, I was just so angry. It was like the child king was with me, lending me his strength." Tera said, looking at her skin and noticing that there seemed to be a little more of a glimmer to it now.

The screams in the halls still continued. They weren't safe yet. Tera truly felt exhausted as Kaiden helped her onto her feet.

"We need to keep going." Kaiden said, as the sound of approaching footsteps filled the hall.

Five orderlies stood before them blocking their exit.

"Well, well, what do we have here? A few stragglers." One of the men in white chuckled, to himself, as the others readied their fists.

Kaiden strode forward, leaving the girls to his back. He hated being useless. He hated letting the others defend him. It left him feeling weak.

"Okay, Crying Girl, if your kind can do this for Tera, then do it for me, too." Kaiden muttered under his breath. He felt desperate for this nightmare to end. The experiments, the torture, all of it. He just wanted peace. They just wanted peace. His vision cleared, and the weariness seemed to drain away from his body. Strength flowed back into his body.

"Let's do this." The orderly on the left said, as he charged Kaiden, who easily dodged the punch with a sidestep.

As one of the other men tried to grab Kaiden by the shoulders, he ducked and swung a hard punch that landed with a loud crack on the man's jaw. The man crumpled to the floor, his jaw had been torn away from the rest of his skull. Blood seeped on the ground as the man twitched a few times, then stopped.

"Alright. Super strength it is." Kaiden laughed to himself, as the other four orderlies seemed to regard him with some caution now.

"Protect them the way I couldn't protect my king." The voice of the crying girl seemed to whisper to Kaiden as he approached the orderlies.

The other men started backing away from Kaiden as he began to rush them.

"Out of the way, weaklings." A booming voice said, as large hands seemed to shove the other orderlies to the side.

"I'll take care of these." The lump that stepped between the orderlies and Kaiden looked like it had once been a man. The thing was large, almost as big as a Silore. It's skin seemed to have dark mist leaking from it and taken on a grey cast, and its body seemed like a balloon that had too much air in it.

The thing bellowed a loud bark of a laugh as

it swung and landed one large fist into Kaiden's gut. The impact of the hit, even with Kaiden's new-found strength, knocked him backwards into the three girls. Kaiden coughed, and wiped his mouth as a small bit of blood had trickled down.

"Stand back. I've got this one." Kaiden said to the girls as the beast charged him. The girls stepped back into an alcove for safety.

"Come and get me you, freak!" Kaiden said, as the Silore beast howled. When it was two steps away from him, Kaiden spun on one foot, kicking up the dusty remains of the Silores that Tera had scorched.

The ash went flying into the thing's eyes. It let out a loud screech as Kaiden spun into the air, connecting his foot with its face. Its head whipped to the side as it fell, grabbing Kaiden by the arm and pulling him down to the ground with it.

"We have to help him." Yun said desperately.

"You're right, Yun. We can't just sit here and wait to see who ends up the victor." Tera said, watching the Silore thing pound on Kaiden, creating a large dent in the ground.

Nora nodded, and orange fire like two miniature suns began to form in her hands. The alcove became bathed in orange glow and heat.

"Let's do this." Nora said, as she strode out of their hiding spot.

"Hey, Ugly!" Nora yelled.

The Silore thing looked up with a grunt, holding Kaiden in its too-large hands.

"Have a taste of this!" Nora growled, as the two orange balls of fire shot towards the beast. It was engulfed in fire instantly. It screamed as it ran in circles, trying to put out the flames. Soon it crumpled into a charred mass. Kaiden coughed as he crawled out of the hole.

"Are you okay?!" Yun exclaimed, as she ran towards Kaiden, who was slightly bloody, but mostly only dirty.

"Yeah. Thank you, Nora, for helping me out there." He said, smiling at Nora.

"You're welcome." Nora said blushing.

"What do you think the Surface will be like?" Yun said, excitedly. The large grate was before them.

A large rusted sign hung on it, *"Personnel Keep Out."*

CHAPTER 7

"How exactly are we supposed to open this thing?" Yun said, kicking the metal gate softly with a clank. The screams had died down.

They assumed everyone they had ever known was now dead. After the thrill of the fight and the adrenaline had calmed down, reality seemed to kick in. Depression and grief fell over the group.

A dark rust, like dried blood, covered most of the grate. There were also drainage marks and debris from years past. Why no one had bothered to clean it up baffled Tera. She knew she was just nitpicking. Nora had already tried to melt the grate, but all that she could muster were pathetic sparks. It was either an emotional power, or it had a time limit. They didn't know, and didn't have time to wait around.

The Silores that had murdered the rest of the Colonists had gathered now, a slowly approaching dark mass, like a storm gathering on the distant horizon.

"What do we do? We've tried everything. All

of these abilities seem to have a freakin' time limit." Nora said, frustrated, as she slumped to the ground, staring at her still-sparkling hands.

Kaiden had tried to lift the grate, but his strength seemed to be exhausted.

Yun paced nervously. She looked at her companions and the gathering Silore army. She had to do something. But what? She didn't seem to have powers like the rest of them.

The Silores began to cackle and yell. One of them threw a dead orderly towards them. The body hit the grate with a loud crash. The force of the throw had not only broken bones in the corpse, but it had dented the grate. Just awesome. Now it really wouldn't open. The body bounced of the ground and rolled a few feet away from them. The girls screamed from the shock of it.

"Give up, half breeds. Your kind lost the war. It is best for you all to be extinct, like the rest of Aelores." The lead Silore spoke, and the others seemed to echo the same resonating message.

The voices filled the hallway, bouncing off of the walls. Yun covered her ears, even though it was in her mind as well. Some type of telepathy, she figured. She had known of one other creature that spoke like that: *The Wolf.*

She could see it now in her mind, covered in

blood and feathers that looked as if it was a galaxy all its own. Its eyes were mismatched indigo and amethyst. She hadn't seen the creature since that day. She thought it was just a delusion, but if these aliens made of smoke and stars were real, then maybe so was The Wolf. She assumed it wasn't probably a wolf, not like she knew it from the articles and books she had read, but just that it was what seemed the closest to it in her mind.

She looked to her companions. They were tired. Tired of fighting.

"I want to fight. I need to help." Yun thought to herself.

The Silores got closer.

"We have to keep fighting." Kaiden said, through gritted teeth.

Tera and Nora wearily got to their feet. Pathetic sparks shot out of Nora's fingertips, and Tera could barely produce a small glow through her body. Kaiden was shaky on his feet.

They all looked exhausted. Yun wished she could feel the same. She was tired, but that was just from lack of sleep. The others were from fighting so hard.

The first Silore had reached them. It charged

as Kaiden rushed out with mildly less enthusiasm as before. His punch was weaker, and it barely moved the alien's head. The Silore chuckled to itself.

"That tickles." It spoke, as it landed a punch on Kaiden, sending him crashing back into the grate, which groaned with from strain. Kaiden didn't move. Yun rushed to his side, as Nora and Tera rushed into the mass of Silores.

"Kaiden!" Yun shouted, as she rushed to him. His breathing was shallow. He appeared to be unconscious. She watched as Nora and Tera fell just as fast as Kaiden did.

The Silores quickly turned their starry eyes on her.

"Whats wrong, child? Not going to fight? Half-breed." The main Silore hissed, as it slowly sauntered closer to Yun.

Half-breed. That was it. She was just like her friends who had powers, too. The power of the Aelore. Though unlike her fiends, Yun had never seen a person made up of stars, or had an experience like Nora.

Yun had *The Wolf.* She wasn't sure how to even begin to summon the thing. All she knew was that she had to do something, or else they would end up like everyone else in the colony.

Steeling herself, she stood up to meet the Silore. There were countless dozens of them now. They had almost swallowed up all of the light in the hall. The only notable light was the stars that shimmered like dying galaxies in their bodies.

"Brave for a half breed who is all alone." It said, mockingly as it stood toe to toe with Yun.

"I am not alone." Yun said with determination. Staring the beast in its unblinking six starry eyes, she waited.

The Silore looked around and laughed. The laugh sounded like screeching metal. The other Silores had caught up with the main one now.

They stood in front of her like a wall. A black solid wall. In one swift move, the Silore swooped up Yun into one of its four arms, its hand wrapped around her neck. It slowly began to choke her. She gasped, clawing at her throat and the Silores' hand, trying to do something.

This wasn't how it was supposed to go. Why couldn't she help, too? Where were the Aelores? Wasn't she a half breed like the Silore had said? Where were her powers?

The world began to grow dark. Her vision began to blur as her lungs burned without air. The little light around her began to shrink, turning into a small pin prick.

She was dying. She knew it.

One of the Silores bellowed. Yun could feel her body flung like a rag doll. She bounced off the ground and rolled. She coughed hard. Blinking through blurry eyes, she could see something in front of her. Something made up of oranges and purples and blues. Something not human in shape. Something she had only ever seen once before in her life.

"You came." Yun croaked, as the Aelore wolf tore into the rest of the Silores. Breaking the line, more wolves followed it. There were three in total. They began killing the Silores, one by one.

"We are here for you, Yun." The larger of the three wolf beasts spoke to her in her mind. Tears welled up in her eyes.

"You came!" Yun cried as tears streamed down her face, while the beasts tore into the Silores.

In only a few minutes, the Silore army had been destroyed, and the hall was now empty, except for the four humans at the grate. The others began to stir. Yun ran to them.

"I'm so glad you guys are alright!" Yun exclaimed.

Tera sat up. All she could see was smoke in the air and three six-legged-dog shaped things walking away from them.

"What was that all about?" She thought to herself.

"What happened to the army?" Kaiden asked.

Yun looked around, seeing that the wolf things had disappeared just like they had appeared. There one moment, and then gone. She shrugged.

"We got a miracle." Yun said, with teary eyes.

"I guess we did." Kaiden said, with a smile.

"Ugh, everything hurts." Nora whined, dusting herself off.

A loud squealing noise suddenly came from the grate. The four of them jumped back as the grate began to slowly open.

"What the heck?" Tera said to herself.

In front of them stood a man in dusty overalls with an equally dirty face. Behind him shone a light none of them had seen before. The light was a mix of oranges and pinks. From what

Tera had read, it was the dawning sun. The dawn of a new day.

"Oscar said you'd come. It only opens on this side." Tobias said, staring at them. There was strange glint in his eyes and an almost evil smile.

"Bring them, in Tobias. Let's see how much they know." A voice whispered to Tobias, like breaking glass. Tobias smiled his dull smile.

"Well, come on now, before anyone else shows up." Tobias waved them up the slope.

The four of them chatted, eagerly as they followed the strange man into the farm. Tera smiled to herself. Kaiden winked at her, and she blushed. Everything was going to work out, she just knew it. She felt bad about all of the dead colonists, but they would thrive for those who died by Silore hands.

They were going to the surface. Oscar would be pleased. Feeling a peace she hadn't felt in a long time, Tera shoved her hand in her pockets. She felt something crumple against her hand. Curious she pulled it out. The paper's title read:

Project Beyond the Stars
The Aelore experiments.
Oscar Ward and James Ward.

The blood stained paper reminded Tera that the momentary peace couldn't last.

CONTINUED IN

THE AELORE TOMES
BOOK 2:

PROJECT BEYOND THE STARS

Vivifica
Studios

AVAILABLE ON AMAZON.COM
VIVIFICASTUDIOS.COM

THE TIMELESS ZODIAC BOOK 1

THE TIMELESS ZODIAC BOOK I

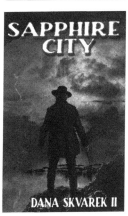

SAPPHIRE CITY

THE VAMPIRE

Jolene Skvarek

ABOUT THE AUTHOR

Jolene Skvarek is an avid reader, comic artist, mangaka and author. Though "Eyes of the Galaxy" is her first published literary work, she has many more soon to come. She lives in Arizona with her husband, Dana Skvarek II, who is another author of several books at Vivifica Studios.

58563205R00066

Made in the USA
Middletown, DE
09 August 2019